I0646584

The extraordinary tales of

Queenie Alice Moon

Queenie's Secret Adventure

Jo Brothers
Illustrated by Lovee

The Extraordinary Tales of Queenie Alice Moon - Queenie's Secret Adventure

Second Printing, 2015
Text and Artwork Copyright © 2015 Jo Brothers
ISBN 978-0-9941093-0-9

Published by:
Perpetuity Media
PO Box 4444
Shortland Street
Auckland
New Zealand 1140

www.perpetuitymedia.com

Published in New Zealand

Printed in the United States of America

Everyone has
extraordinary tales to tell.

This book is dedicated to

you.

Queenie woke up early that morning, it was a beautiful day and the sun shone brightly into her bedroom.

The light caught the crystal chandeliers so that they cast a maze of snowflake patterns on the walls and roof.

Pugnatius was asleep at the end of Queenie's bed and he did not hear her get up and quietly sneak out of the room.

On such a glorious day as this Queenie decided she wanted a secret adventure out to visit the Fairy Queen, Bluebelle.

Bluebelle was a great friend of Queenie's and she was also an excellent teacher about the secrets of herbs and natural potions.

It was thanks to Bluebelle's herb medicine that Moonbeam got help to cure his case of unicorn measles.

He was covered in rainbow coloured spots and it was only after eating a large amount of Angelica plant that his lovely ivory white hair reapperaed and he was back to his usual handsome self.

As Queenie snuck out and along the hall of Magic she checked to see Moonbeam and Yang fast asleep outside her bedroom, they were her fantastic royal guardians and kept her safe.

Queenie wanted to be able to share more and to learn more about herb magic so she could help her family and friends.

Quietly she opened the Palace door and closed it behind her. She looked to make sure no one had heard her and bent down to pick up a picnic basket she had hidden last night, from behind the red rose bush at the Palace door.

Queenie was walking quickly and soon felt the need to stop and sit under the shade of a large willow tree by the Wishing Well pond and eat a small cake for nourishment.

In keeping with tradition Queenie threw a gold coin into the pond and made a wish. "I am safe, I am well and I am off to Bluebelle."

With that she threw the coin deep into the pond and did not notice a parrot sitting watching her in the shadows.

Bluebelle lived in the Crimson Valley where the army of evil flying snakes had recently tried to steal happiness.

As she walked through the forest, the tall trees made it darker and darker and she wished she had Pugnatius, Yang and Moonbeam with her because together friends can do anything.

Feeling brave she stepped forward onto a black slippery looking stick. The stick moved, wings shot out and it turned to face Queenie. An evil flying snake was staring into Queenie's eyes.

"Get away from me you beast!", Queenie said bravely.

"Actually it's Admiral Serpentine to you, Queenie!"

Queenie literally looked into the face of darkness, Admiral Serpentine was in charge of the army of evil flying snakes.

It was in this moment that all of Queenie's mind power training came into effect. Queenie had been taught from a young age that what you think is the reality that you create.

Another understanding is that any test you get, you have the strength to overcome it.

Queenie was not afraid, she had certainty that she was safe and that Admiral Serpentine was the one who should be afraid.

Meanwhile back at the palace, Pugnatius woke up, he felt in his heart that something was happening to Queenie.

"Moonbeam, Yang, quickly come in here! Where is Queenie?", Pugnatius yelled. Moonbeam and Yang quickly flew into Queenie's bedroom and looked at each other.

"How did she manage to leave without us knowing?" Yang asked. "Now is not the time for questions, we need answers!", Moonbeam said as he stomped his hoof.

Pugnatius saw a piece of paper on the floor by Queenie's bed and read it out loud.

"Reminder - Get picnic basket to take to the Wishing Well'.

Quick everyone, she is at the Wishing Well. We must go and find her at once!" They all rushed out the door and ran across the Palace gardens.

Pugnatius, Moonbeam and Yang soon arrived at the Wishing Well pond and were disappointed that they couldn't see Queenie anywhere.

A colourful parrot flew up to sit on Moonbeam's back. He had a red ribbon in his mouth and he kept repeating, "I am safe, I am well, and I am off to Bluebelle."

"What luck, an echo parrot! Queenie must have been here because he has a ribbon from her dress and she is off to see Bluebelle in the Crimson Valley." said Moonbeam.

Back in the dark forest Queenie and Admiral Serpentine were still staring at each other.

Queenie saw a forked branch hanging from a tree, she knew if she reached out and grabbed the tree she could pin Admiral Serpentine's head to the ground and he would be powerless.

Queenie had certainty that she could do this, she knew that certainty is achieved by moving forward despite how things may appear.

With a puff of magical yellow mist Queenie had used the forked branch to pin Admiral Serpentine to the ground.

Admiral Serpentine let out a vile screech, which was the sound of the serpent calling for his army.

The last thing Queenie wanted was an army of evil flying snakes invading Spectrum to rescue the Admiral. So without fear she stuffed a small cake into Admiral Serpentine's mouth.

Queenie heard a sound behind her and turned around to see Pugnatius running toward her with a determined look on his face. He jumped and landed directly on Admiral Serpentine's belly winding him beautifully.

Moonbeam and Yang arrived together to see the sky fill with evil flying snakes.

Queenie gave Moonbeam, Yang and Pugnatius their secret signal that had been developed for just such an occasion.

Once again Queenie activated her magical yellow mist and it surrounded Admiral Serpentine and his army of evil flying snakes who were magnetically drawn to a black hole in the stratosphere.

They were pulled toward the black hole with such force it was as if a huge vacuum cleaner in the sky had been turned on.

Later that evening, Queenie, her parents, Moonbeam, Yang and Pugnatius were having a celebration dinner. "I promise I will never again go out without one of my royal guardians." Queenie said to her parents.

"I am sorry, I just wanted to learn the herb medicine from Bluebelle" and as she said those words there was a twinkling sound.

"Did someone say my name?", Bluebelle asked smiling. "Queenie, I am here to give you your herb lessons, you have such a huge desire to learn about this to help your friends and family that I will give you a lesson once a week."

Queenie was delighted that she had already learnt several big lessons.

Queenie knew she was far stronger than she had known. Queenie knew that we all need to look out for each other and Queenie knew that one day she might help someone and one day they would help her.

About Jo

Jo has a passion for storytelling and writing that started when she was a young girl and continues to this very day. She has a vivid imagination and loves creating new worlds and wonderful characters that burst into life with valour and flamboyance such as Queenie Alice Moon and Nano the Robot.

She equally writes intriguing novelettes with quirky, eccentric characters that are weaved into supernatural themes and in her soon to be released books series, Immortales Excelsus she writes about an ordinary, thoroughly bored teen, Sabra Leon, who discovers she and her family are not so ordinary and that their history has more than a few secrets that date back to the dawn of time.

"Thanks for visiting, happy imagining! "

Please keep in touch with me at www.jobrothers.com

Jo lives in Auckland, New Zealand with her husband Sean, in a home filled with books and imagination.